EGMONT
We bring stories to life

First published in Great Britain 2013 by Egmont UK Limited
The Yellow Building, 1 Nicholas Road, London W11 4AN

© 2009 – 2013 Rovio Entertainment Ltd.
Rovio, Angry Birds, Bad Piggies, Mighty Eagle and
all related titles, logos and characters
are trademarks of Rovio Entertainment Ltd.

ISBN 978 1 4052 6783 0
55146/3
Printed in Italy

Bird spotting!

Your mission, should you choose to accept it, is to seek out special objects hidden in these packed scenes. But before you flock to begin your first task, get to know the main players ...

Red
AKA: Red Bird
Most likely to be found: in the middle of the action – leading from the front!

Terence
AKA: Big Brother
Most likely to be found: hanging about grumpily at the back of the flock!

Jim, Jake and Jay
AKA: the Blues
Most likely to be found: together, of course!

Matilda
AKA: White Bird
Most likely to be found: protecting the eggs.

Chuck
AKA: Yellow Bird
Most likely to be found: wherever pigs need knocking over!

Hal
AKA: Green Bird
Most likely to be found: zooming around, boomerang style!

King Pig
Most likely to be found: hiding behind his subjects. Scaredy-cat ... um ... pig.

Foreman Pig
Most likely to be found: stomping around trying to look important.

Corporal Pig
Most likely to be found: in the middle of the action, getting hit!

Minion Pigs
Most likely to be found: anywhere and everywhere. You just can't seem to shake these porkers!

Construction destruction!

The pigs are busy building their next dastardly construction. See if you can find everything on the list before they clock off.

Jim, Jake and Jay

14 hooks

2 Hals

Summer fun

Phew!

Is it hot in here? The birds are taking a break from tormenting their piggy nemeses to soak up the rays. Hmmm, ever get the feeling you're being watched?

Can you spot:

6 spying pigs

8 strawberries

5 Reds with sunglasses

Pigs might fly!

Those pigs will hide anywhere to get away from the birds, even above the clouds! Keep your head high and don't look down!

Can you spot:

3 minions with pink snouts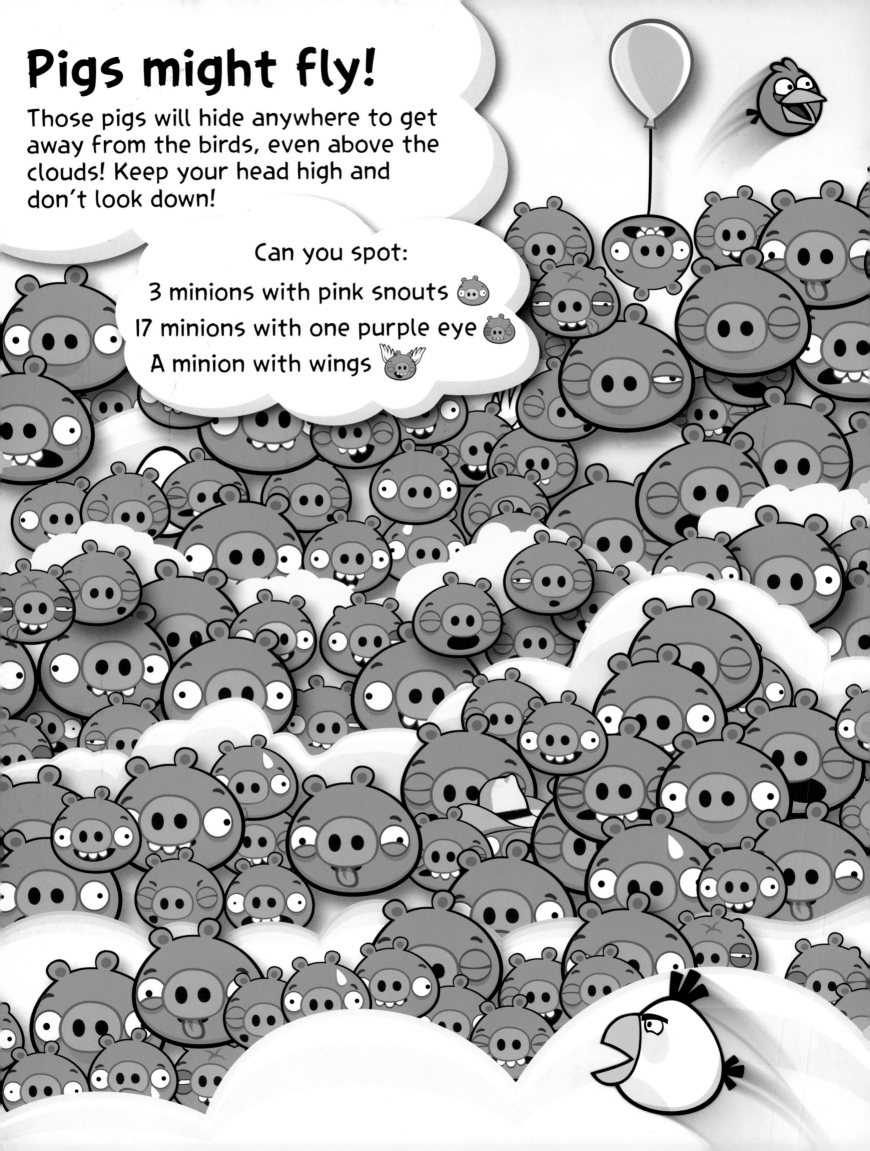

17 minions with one purple eye

A minion with wings

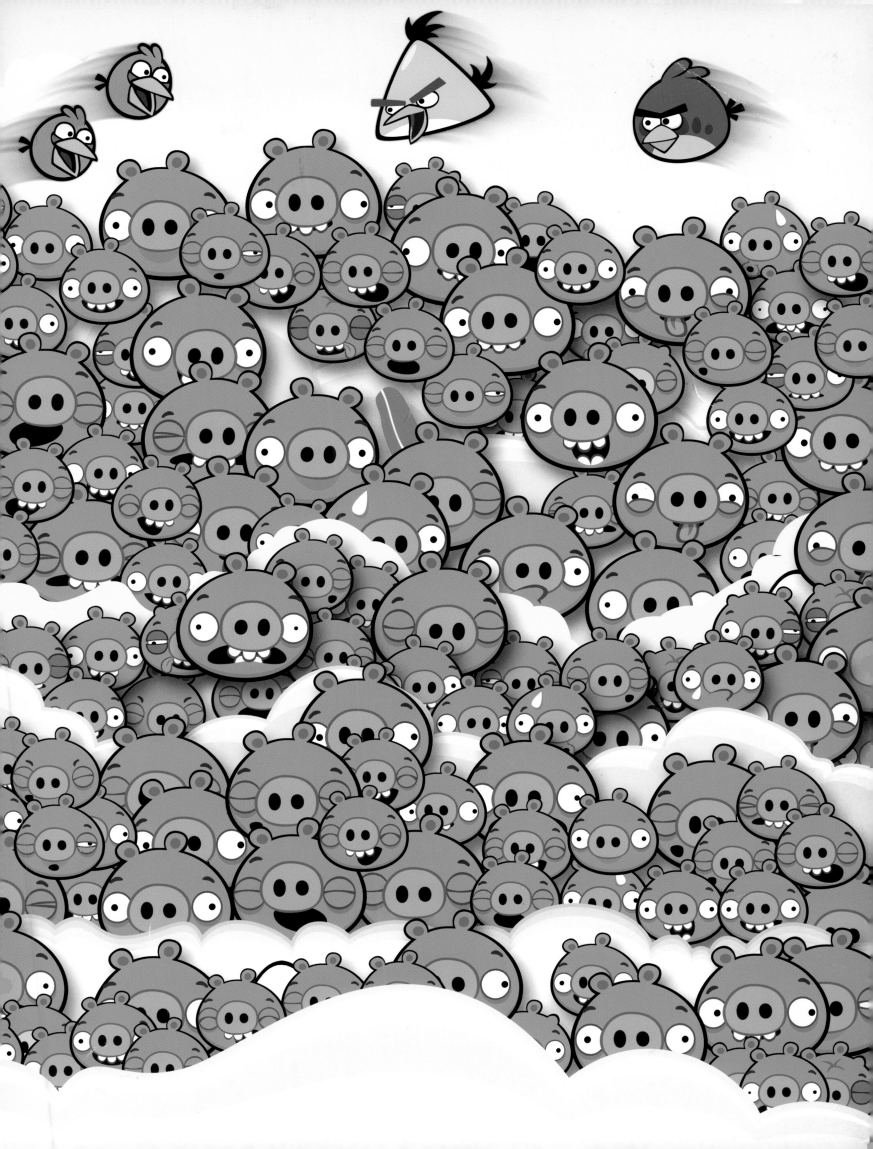

Who turned out the lights?

Shhh! It's night time and the birds and pigs have called a truce to get some shut eye ... or have they? Tiptoe round the page and get searching!

Can you find:

King Pig

20 minions with one eye open

7 spades

Seeing Red

See if you can find the
following in this explosion
of red bird goodness!

10 Reds with a red beak

10 red balloons

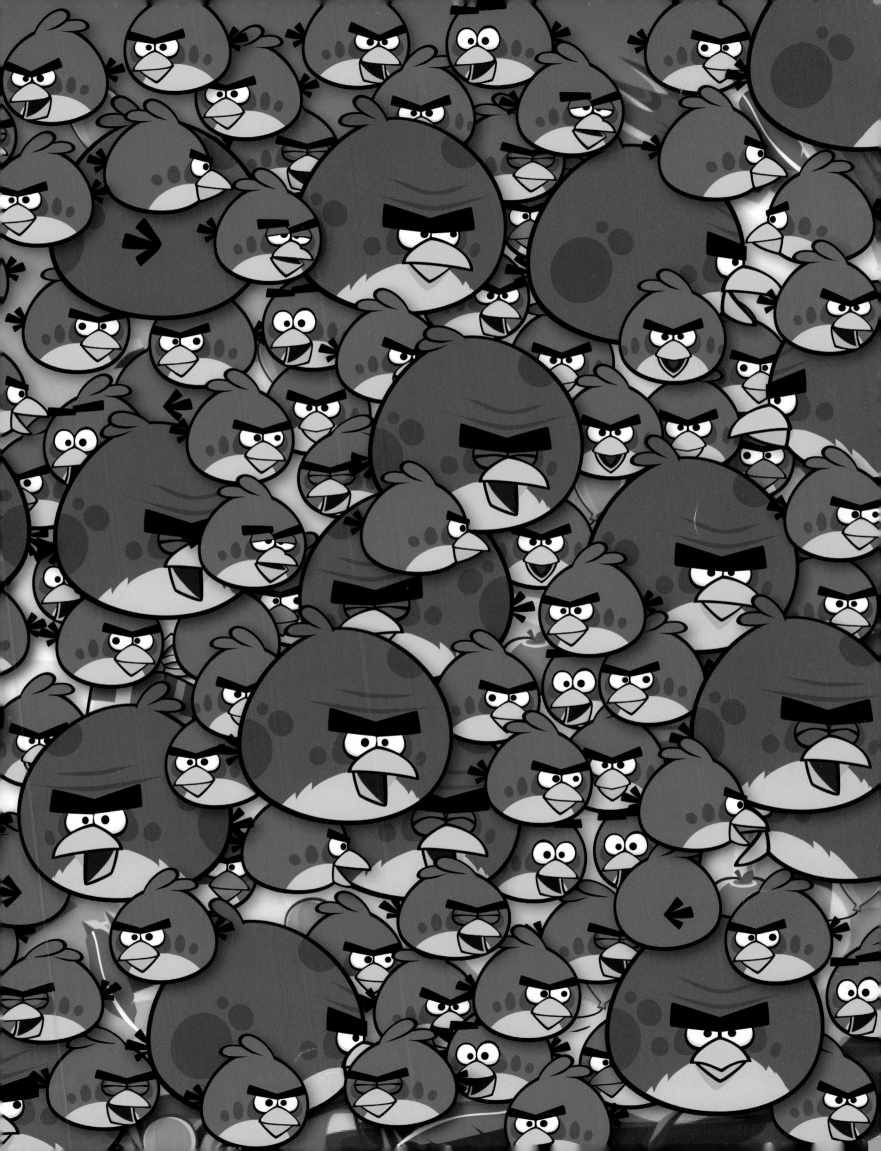

Cave dwellers

The pigs have taken their stolen loot underground!

Can you spot:

8 miner pigs

8 blue birds

8 Red miners

Hurry, before the rest of the Angry Birds flock into the cave!

Happy Porkmas!

Ah, it's that special time of year when angry differences are put aside and goodwill to all birds and pigs is shared ... Yeah, right!

Can you find:

4 frozen pigs

Red with an ice cream

6 candy canes

Angry apocalypse!

The Angry Birds are out of control! Can you count how many of each bird appear on the page?

What else can you spot?

Flip back through the book to find more stuff!

Construction destruction!

A minion with a special helmet badge

5 pickaxes

Chuck

Summer fun

6 doughnuts

One blue bird with a blue beak

Red with one eyebrow

Pigs might fly!

A pig with a hat

3 eggs

A green feather

Who turned out the lights?

8 yellow stars

A minion standing on his head

Terence

Seeing Red

6 red apples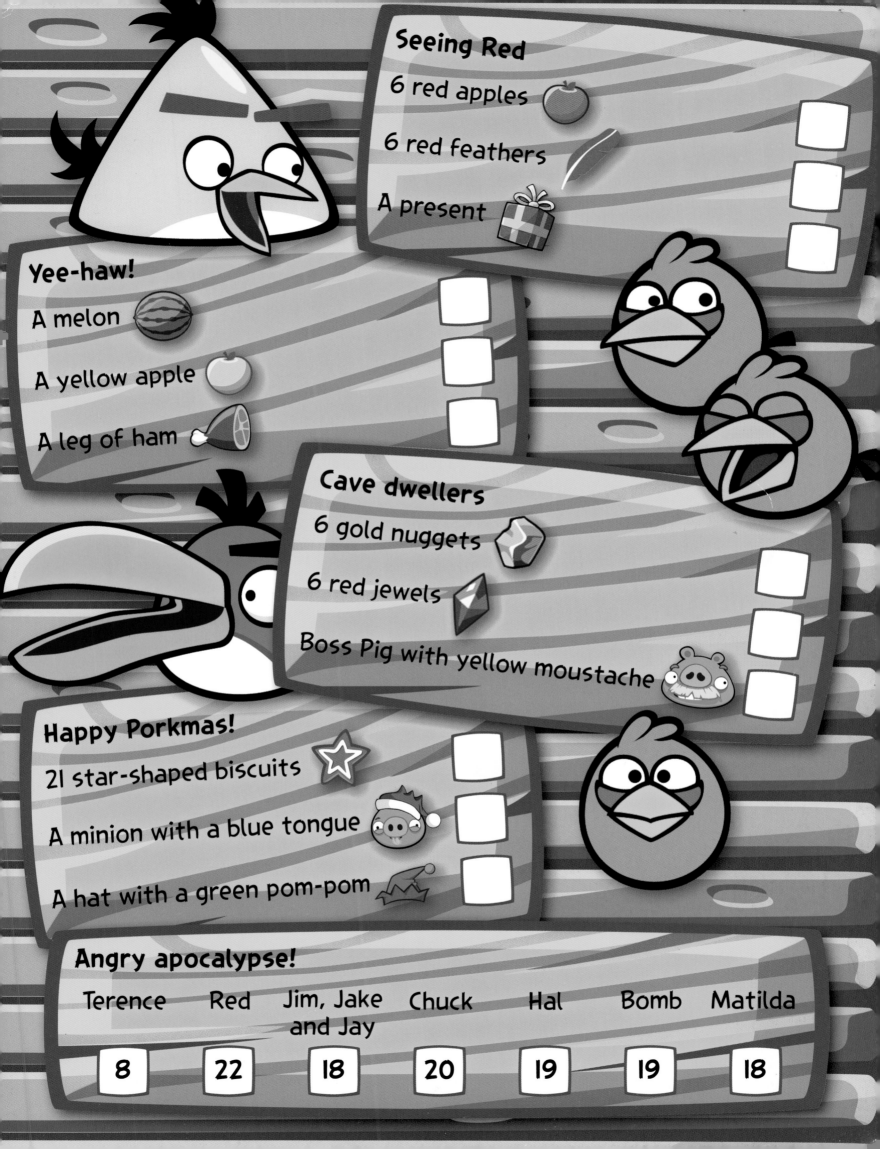

6 red feathers

A present

Yee-haw!

A melon

A yellow apple

A leg of ham

Cave dwellers

6 gold nuggets

6 red jewels

Boss Pig with yellow moustache

Happy Porkmas!

21 star-shaped biscuits

A minion with a blue tongue

A hat with a green pom-pom

Angry apocalypse!

Terence	Red	Jim, Jake and Jay	Chuck	Hal	Bomb	Matilda
8	22	18	20	19	19	18

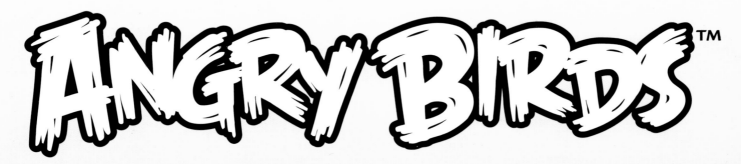